Disney
MINNIE

Where's Fifi?

Minnie Mouse and Fifi were having a lovely walk when Minnie spotted a banner. "How exciting!" said Minnie. "A dog show right here in the park! Fifi, wouldn't you like to enter?"

DOG SHOW!
THIS SATURDAY AT NOON
IN THE PARK
PRIZES!

As soon as they got home, Minnie and Fifi started practicing for the show. Fifi remembered how to sit and shake a paw, but when Minnie said "Roll over!" Fifi sat up and barked.

"Silly Fifi," Minnie laughed. "I said 'roll over'! When I want you to sit up and bark, I'll say 'bark'!" Fifi wagged her tail and rolled onto her back. She wanted a tummy rub.

On Saturday morning, before the dog show, Minnie gave Fifi a bath, a brushing, and a polka-dot bow. Fifi may not have understood all of Minnie's commands, but she looked lovely!

On the way to the park Fifi spotted a squirrel. She loved chasing squirrels!

"Fifi, heel!" cried Minnie, but Fifi was too excited to listen. She wiggled and squirmed until her collar slipped off. The squirrel ran around the corner with Fifi in hot pursuit.

"Fifi, stay!" cried Minnie as Fifi bounded away.

Minnie ran as fast as she could, but by the time she had turned the corner, there was no sign of Fifi. "Fifi! Here, Fifi!" cried Minnie as she searched the street.

Minnie phoned Daisy.
"Fifi is lost!"

"I'm on my way,"
promised Daisy.

Daisy picked up Mickey on her way over. The two of them had a plan. "Don't worry Minnie, we'll find her!" said Mickey. "I hope so!" Minnie sniffled, "I miss her already!"

Daisy called the animal shelter and gave them a description of Fifi. "She's freshly groomed and wearing a polka-dot bow!"

Then they bought some art supplies so that they could make posters and let everyone know that they were looking for a missing dog.

Making the posters made them
feel more hopeful.

They put up posters all over town, calling "Here, Fifi!" as
they worked.

When they were done they headed back to Minnie's house in case Fifi had found her way home. "Thanks for all your help," Minnie said.

Fifi wasn't at the house. "Oh dear. I don't know what to do!" said Minnie.

"She'll turn up!" Mickey promised.

Daisy took out her phone. "I'm posting a message to ask all my friends to help us find Fifi."

Fifi is lost! Please help us find her. She's small, with tan and cream fur, and she's wearing a polka-dot bow. Please message me if you see her!

"That's got to work," smiled Mickey.

"It just might!" said Minnie.

Messages started coming in almost immediately.

I'll go out and look!

Poor thing, I'll keep an eye out.

Sure thing, Daisy!

Is this Fifi?

Then a picture appeared. It was of a tan and cream dog with a polka-dot bow and a big blue ribbon!

"Fifi! That's my Fifi!" cried Minnie. Daisy sent a message back asking where they had found the dog. When the answer came, Minnie set off at a run for the park with Mickey and Daisy close behind.

Fifi barked happily when she spotted Minnie.
Minnie hugged her. Fifi gave Minnie lots of kisses.

"Oh Fifi, I was so worried!" Minnie exclaimed. "What are you doing here? Why are you wearing this ribbon?"

"Your dog is so well behaved," said one of the judges. "She sits when she's told and she knows how to shake a paw. She's so smart! We all agreed that she deserved to win!"

Minnie whispered in Fifi's ear,
"Good thing they didn't ask you to roll over!"
Fifi sat up and barked. Minnie laughed,
glad to know her prize-winning dog was
safe and sound!